That's My House

THAT'S
My HOUSE
Possess The Land

DR. REGINA MURRAY

XULON PRESS

Xulon Press
2301 Lucien Way #415
Maitland, FL 32751
407.339.4217
www.xulonpress.com

Illustrated by: Ahmad Jones

Paperback ISBN-13: 978-1-66286-415-5
Hard Cover ISBN-13: 978-1-66286-416-2
Ebook ISBN-13: 978-1-66286-417-9

Now therefore, behold,
the cry of the children …. Exodus 3:9 (KJV)

This book is dedicated to my grandchildren
and to all children, parents, and elders who
realize that it is never too early or too late to
dream of homeownership.

That's your house…Possess the Land.

Chapter One

The school bus drove slowly down Cascade Road, filled with the chatter of middle schoolers who were elated that only five weeks were left in the school year.

Anaya, Amari, Reggie, and Yvette lived in the same neighborhood and had been the best of friends since kindergarten.

They always made sure to sit together on the bus to and from school every day.

And as if that wasn't enough, they were always together on the weekends too.

Anticipating a homework-free summer, the mood was very joyful on the bus.

Then a shout erupted. "That's my house, that's my house!" said Amari.

"You called that one last week!" yelled Anaya.

Well," said Amari, "that's my dreeaaaam house," making sure to drag the word out slowly for emphasis, as he often did, "so I'm gonna keep claiming that one every week!"

Yvette chimed in, "So, how about I just buy the whole block so you can't say that's your house anymore?"

"Wait a minute, one person can't buy a whole block!" Amari protested.

"Yes, they can. They can buy a whole bunch of houses and then rent them to other people who need somewhere to live. That's what landlords do," explained Yvette.

"Okay, okay…this is all just for fun and games, right?" Anaya interjected. "Let's just keep pretending. It's exactly like playing Monopoly but without the board, characters, and little toy houses."

"Like I said, I'm buying the whoooole block… okay!" Yvette declared while laughing, mimicking Amari's long, drawn-out way of speaking.

Reggie joined the banter. "Okay, so I see that we have leveled up! If you're buying a whole block, I'm buying me some acres." Getting into thinking mode, Reggie continued, "Let's see… how many houses can you put on five acres?"

Yvette had a change of heart. "Nah, I don't need the whole block...one house is enough for me—one *big* house."

"All right, calm down, game over!" yelled the bus driver, Mr. Gray. "Everybody out! We're at your stop."

Mr. Gray secretly loved to hear the children get so excited as they talked about houses. It reminded him that he too had played this game as a child with his siblings. *Ah, what memories,* he thought, smiling. *"That's my house."* *Yes, it's not too late.*

"Bye…Bye…See ya!" The children began scattering in separate directions, swinging their backpacks and having those last-minute conversations before leaving their friends.

Amari, still laughing loudly, yelled out from a distance, "I'm still calling for my same house tomorrow! I loooove that neighborhood! I dream about that house every single night."

Anaya yelled back, "Tomorrow is Saturday—there's no school, silly! You will be by yourself."

"Well, Monday then. Bye!" said Amari.

Chapter Two

The weekend sped by quickly, as weekends usually do.

Monday, on the bus ride home, the friends were at it again.

Amari said, "Hey, Reggie, why are you so quiet? We are about to pass by your faaaaaaavorite house. Aren't you getting ready to yell out, 'That's my house!'?"

Reggie sighed deeply. "Yeah, but I was seriously daydreaming about us living in our own house all weekend long. Man, that would be so fun. I mean, all weekend long. I even talked to my mom about it. Then while we were going grocery shopping Sunday, we passed by this house on Niskey Lake, and I was like, 'Wow. Now that could be my house for real!'"

Amari laughed. "What did your mom say? I bet she said, 'Boy, if you don't stop all of that daydreaming!'"

"No way," Reggie replied. "She got really quiet for a moment and then said, 'If you and your friends are serious about it, you should start planning.' She said we can still play our 'That's my house' game, but we should also start planning for our future."

"Planning?" Yvette laughed. "Are you serious? Hmm...I mean, this is our last year in middle school, but...you're not even a man yet."

Reggie responded, "But I will be in a few years. My mom said it's never too early to start planning for our future. That's what she and my dad have actually been working on for us. A house of our own, can you believe it? She was planning to surprise me and my little sister with the news, but she got so hyped when she saw my excitement as we drove past those nice brick homes. We are *finally* moving from our tiny apartment. Yes!"

"Wow!" exclaimed Anaya, "my mom needs to talk to your parents and find out what they had to do. We want a house too. My parents daydream about houses all the time just like we do. The only difference is, they don't yell out, 'That's my house!'" The children laughed. "But we do talk about it as a family while we're having dinner on Sundays. They say it's really hard to buy a house without having tons of money. But there's got to be a way. I mean, I see a lot of other people living in their own houses. What's up with that?"

"Well, count us in too," said Yvette and Amari simultaneously. "We wanna know what to do!"

"Once I started asking questions, my mom was on a roll," Reggie said. "She started talking *way* above my head. Talking about building ge-ne-ra ...something. Wait, yeah...generational wealth."

"Ge-ne what?" said Anaya, Amari, and Yvette in unison.

"What exactly is ge-ne-ra-tion-al wealth?" asked Amari. "I know what wealth or wealthy means. I had those words on my vocabulary test. But, um, you lost me with that big word."

"Well, I guess I'm gonna have to take you to school right quick!" said Reggie. "If you already know what wealth and wealthy mean, just add generations to it and put the words together. Generations plus wealth equals generational wealth. So, look, you, your parents, and your grandparents are three generations. Me, my parents, and my grandparents are three generations. Generations basically means the span of time between you and your parents, and in this case, their parents too."

"Got it," said Amari, nodding his head.

Reggie continued, "My mom explained that my grandparents didn't have a lot of money or wealth to pass down to her, but if they had, that would be an example of what generational wealth is. We pass it down to the next generation."

"Ah, it's like they give you a head start for your future," said Amari.

"Okay, I get it now too," said Anaya. "Generational wealth…sounds good to me. I could use some generational wealth!" she said, laughing.

"Trust me," said Reggie, "this was all new to me, so I had loads of questions. I even started writing them down so I wouldn't forget. The way I see it, you guys may have some of the same questions, right? By the way, did you guys notice this note pad that I have with me? I am so serious. I don't want to miss or forget anything. When we finished our errands Sunday and my dad came home from work, my mom and I were still sitting on the sofa, talking about houses. Not to be left out of the conversation, my dad pulled up a chair and joined the conversation. I had just mentioned to my mom how we play "That's My House" on the school bus every single day. Of course, my dad wanted to hear about all the details of the game, so I had to repeat it again. When I finished describing it to them, they looked at one another, and I saw 'the look.' You know, the look that your parents give you when they are getting ready to plan your next move for you?"

"Yeah, we know that look...right guys?" said Anaya. Amari and Yvette nodded their head in agreement.

"Anyway," continued Reggie, "Mom and Dad both agreed that we should start a club and simply call it 'That's My House.'"

"A club?" Yvette asked. "Would we have to pay dues? My allowance is only $20 per month, and I need all of it. I have goals!"

"Yeah, shopping goals!" Anaya snapped back, and they both began to laugh.

"Let me explain," Reggie said. "You won't pay dues to me; you'll pay them to yourself. How about that? It's like investing in yourself... ha, that's something else I learned this weekend—'investing in yourself.' Here's the best part. The dues are only $10 per month, but guess what? My parents are going to match each of our $10, so we will really be saving $20 per month!"

"Wait...hold up," said Yvette as she reached into her backpack. "Where's my calculator? Let's see, 12 months times $20 is how much? Yes! We will be saving $240 a year! Now, I like the sound of that!"

"And, if you decide to save more, they said they'll match that too!" said Reggie.

"Hmm," Amari spoke up, "I have an idea. What if each of us asks our parents to do the same? Every little bit helps, right? I bet they'll say yes to the matching funds piece."

Here came hyper Yvette again, "Now this whole scenario sounds super good! When do we start? Today? Tomorrow? Saturday? I am so excited and ready!"

Reggie laughed and said, "Calm down, girl… calm down."

The bus slowed down at the stop light. "Alright, everybody, get your books and backpacks together!" yelled Mr. Gray.

"Oh my goodness!" laughed Reggie. "We missed all of our 'that's my houses' while actually talking about houses! Now that's funny!"

On the left side of the school bus, something grabbed Anaya's attention. "What street is this? Look at that house on the corner with the wide porch and beautiful hanging plants. I don't remember seeing that one before. See, I guess I am getting more serious now. I can see myself with a house just like that."

"Well, I hope y'all are ready for this club because my parents are quite serious," Reggie warned.

Yvette declared, "I know I am ready! I'm talking T-shirts, baseball caps, coloring books, journals…you name it! Can't you just see it? In neon lights…'That's My House.'"

"Slow down, girl, the club is just getting started!" said Reggie. "But, hold on a minute, that really is a good idea. If we market and sell our club merchandise, we can make extra money to add to our club's bank account!"

Yvette pulled out her trusty calculator as laughter came from the crew, "Make sure it's an interest-bearing savings account!"

"And there she goes!" her friends all chimed in.

"Well, Yvette," said Reggie, "sounds like you want to be the club's treasurer, the 'That's My House' banker. Am I right?"

"I'm fine with that," said Yvette. "You know I love numbers, and not to brag, but I always get A's in pre-algebra!"

"Show off!" said Anaya, and they all laughed.

The conversation continued as Mr. Gray pulled to the curb and opened the bus doors. The children hopped off the bus, still talking. Not once did anyone yell, "That's my house!" on the way home that day, but the wheels were turning, and the light bulbs were coming on as they were making real plans—plans to possess the land.

As the friends continued walking, Reggie, in his new leadership role, gave the command, "Okay, guys and girls, let's get inside, finish our homework, and then daydream and plan some more for our club. Yep, that's my house, that's my house, that's my house," he repeated over and over. "So, are we all set for Saturday at noon? My mom said we can meet at our place. She even said she'll make us lunch!"

"Hope it's pizza!" said Amari. "That's my fave!"

13

"I'll make a special request for pizza for you!" Reggie responded while laughing. "Is that all you ever eat, Amari?"

CHAPTER THREE

The rest of the week flew by, and the other children on the bus noticed a shift in the conversations between Reggie, Anaya, Amari, and Yvette. All they talked about were houses, but in quieter tones than before. No more yelling out, "That's my house!" in a game-like manner. They seemed really focused. But periodically, one of them would glance up and let out a quick, "That's my house!" It was as if they had matured over a period of three weeks.

As things wound down to the end of the school year, their vocabulary had seemingly changed. After attending a few of the "That's My House" weekend club meetings, their conversations on the school bus were more about various styles of houses, bank accounts, real estate agents, and even credit scores.

"Reggie, your mom is amazing! I can't believe how much we have learned in three weekends. I feel…what's the word I'm looking for? Empowered. Yeah, that's it!" said the usually quiet Amari.

"We are empowered!" Reggie boasted. "Once you gain this kind of knowledge, you can do things, make moves. Like they say in text talk, 'If You Know, You Know.'"

Yvette, the thinker, got really quiet, then said, "What about the kids who don't have someone like Reggie's mom to teach them? Man, that just doesn't seem fair. They will miss out on so much as they grow up. They really should be teaching this stuff in school."

"You are absolutely right!" said Anaya. "Why don't we learn this in school? I am just glad that someone cared enough to share this knowledge with us. But wait a minute, guys, guess what? Guess who has decided to start an adult version of the 'That's My House' club? My parents!"

"What?" exclaimed Reggie. "Wait until I tell my mom and dad! That's what I'm talking about! Each one teach one. We have started something great, I see."

Amari said, "Yep, it's gonna be spreading like wildfire now. Sounds like everyone wants and deserves a home of their own. We have to keep this club going even through high school and college so that it happens for more families."

"So, are y'all still writing your goals and dreams in your journals between our meetings like we said we would?" asked Anaya. "Accountability, now, accountability. Like my preacher said in his sermon last Sunday, 'Write the vision and make it plain.'"

"Amen," said Amari, raising his hands and waving them like he was in church.

"I'm doing more than that," said Reggie. "I am drawing pictures of the inside of my dream home, making a list of what kind of furniture I want in my man cave…yep, that's right, me and my dad are gonna have the nicest man cave ever!"

"Okay, Reggie, so that means me and Yvette can start planning for our pink and green she-sheds in our back yards!" said Anaya while laughing.

"Wait a minute," said Yvette, "mine has to be red, girl!"

Anaya rolled her eyes, "Oh yeah, I forgot both of our aunties are always talking about that sorority thing!"

The girls then did the secret sorority hand signals and laughed out loud.

"Whatever you want...dream about it, talk about, pray about it, draw pictures of it, make a vision board, pick out your paint colors—go for it all!" said Reggie.

Yvette jumped up, re-energized, "That's the part I am excited about, decorating my own house the way I want to, not the way the landlord says we have to! 'Don't hang pictures on the wall...don't paint the walls bold colors...don't hang plants on the fence...yada yada yada...I mean, come on!"

Anaya laughed and gave Yvette a high five, "You know it!"

Regina Murray

Suddenly, Reggie yelled out, "That's my house on the next block! Whoa, slow down, Mr. Gray! It's right there on the corner of Danforth and Cascade!"

The bus started slowing down. The stop light gave Reggie more time to excitedly share his news.

Anaya, Yvette, and Amari all laughed. "Man, Reggie, you're still daydreaming!" said Amari. "Quit playing."

"No, seriously," said Reggie, "I wanted to surprise y'all. We moved this past weekend. My mom and dad finished buying the house. They called it 'closing the escrow' or something like that. They even took me with them to the appointment Friday, where they signed about a million pieces of paper...well, maybe fifty pieces of paper. We had to go to an attorney's office. I met the real estate agent who helped them find the house. She was pretty cool. She even talked to the seller of the house for them and helped them with all of those papers...whew!"

Laughing, Reggie continued, "I had to put on my church suit and everything for that appointment. Whatever it was called, we got our keys... and that's our house! I told y'all these club meetings worked! I have so much more to tell you guys. I learned a major lesson at home this week that I will talk about at our next meeting. Which

will now be held, drumroll please…in the base-
ment of our brand-new house! Yes!"

"Talk about a crash course and a bunch of new
vocabulary words," Reggie continued. "My brain
was in overdrive. It felt like I was already in high
school or even college. When my mom told the
realtor what she was teaching us in our club, the
realtor said we basically have an on-going first-
time homebuyer seminar. She thought that was
an amazing way to pay it forward in our com-
munity. The thing is, my mom laid down the
facts in a way that even as a kid, I could under-
stand, plus she told me how they were able to
accomplish becoming homeowners, step by step.
She kept reminding me that although it didn't
happen overnight, planning made all the difference in the world. My mom said number one:
save your money for a down payment. Shout out
to our club for getting a head start on saving!

Number two: make sure you pay all the
people you owe on time. You know, like credit
cards and stuff. Because apparently, your credit
score is something that banks look at when you
want to get a loan.

Number three: get to know the people at the
bank so you can get a loan or mortgage when
you are ready to buy your house.

Number four: you want to know a reliable real estate agent who can help you. But anyway, I gotta go…we'll talk more about it Saturday. I guess if you handle your personal business right like my mom said, we can all do this!"

As the light turned green, Reggie finally stopped talking and stood up to get off the bus, then turned around to wave bye to his friends.

"So, who's next?" he asked. "Who is going to be next to become a homeowner?"

With hands raised, Anaya, Amari, and Yvette yelled, "Me…me…me!" They looked behind them, and more of the children on the bus had their hands raised as well.

Echoes of "Me…me…me!" filled the bus. They had been listening all along. *Wow…I guess you never know who is listening and being helped,* thought Reggie.

Mr. Gray glanced around, raised one hand from the steering wheel, and whispered under his breath, "Me too…me too…that's my house! It's not too late."

That's my house. Let's possess the land!

GLOSSARY

https://www.dictionary.com/

All definitions are from dictionary.com except where noted.

Accountability – the state of being accountable, liable, or answerable. Subject to the obligation to report, explain, or justify something.

Acre – a common measure of area: in the U.S. and U.K., 1 acre equals 4,840 square yards (4,047 square meters) or 0.405 hectare; 640 acres equals one square mile.

Appraise(r) –to estimate the monetary value of; determine the worth of; assess: *We had an expert appraise the house before we bought it.*

Attorney- a lawyer; attorney-at-law.

Bank- an institution for receiving, lending, exchanging, and safeguarding money and, in some cases, issuing notes and transacting other financial business.

Bank account-

1. an account with a bank.
2. A balance standing to the credit of a depositor at a bank.

Credit- The term *credit* has several financial meanings, but all of them are based on the confidence and trust that lenders or vendors have in an individual's ability to pay in a timely fashion. (*Credit* is ultimately derived from Latin *crēdere* "to believe, entrust, give credit.")

Credit can involve entrusting a buyer with goods or services without requiring immediate payment. *Credit* can also involve a transaction in which a lender provides financing to a borrower in return for future monthly repayments, usually including interest.

Credit score – A numerical ranking of an individual's financial creditworthiness based on spending and credit history, indicating to potential lenders and credit card issuers the individuals capacity and likelihood to make timely payments o amounts due on loans and credit cards.

Deed- *Law.* a writing or document executed under seal and delivered to effect a conveyance, especially of real estate.

Down payment – an initial up front partial payment for the purchase of expensive items/services such as a car or a house. It is usually paid in cash or equivalent at the time of finalizing the transaction. A loan of some sort is then required to finance the remainder of the payment.

https://en.m.wikipedia.org

Escrow-

1. a contract, deed, bond, or other written agreement deposited with a third person, by whom it is to be delivered to the grantee or promise on the fulfillment of some condition.
2. to place in escrow: *The home seller agrees to escrow the sum of $1000 with his attorney.*

Financial literacy-

FINANCIAL, FISCAL, MONETARY, PECUNIARY refer to matters concerned with money. FINANCIAL usually refers to money matters or transactions of some size or importance:

<u>Literacy</u>–the quality or state of being literate, especially the ability to read and write. A person's knowledge of a particular subject or field: *to acquire computer literacy; improving your financial literacy.*

Generation(al)- the average span of years between the birth of parents and the birth of their offspring. The entire body of individuals born and living at about the same time:

Invest- to put (money) to use, by purchase or expenditure, in something offering potential profitable returns, as interest, income, or appreciation in value.

Insurance- the act, system, or business of insuring property, life, one's person, etc., against loss or harm arising in specified contingencies, as fire, accident, death, disablement, or the like, in consideration of a payment proportionate to the risk involved.

Coverage by contract in which one party agrees to indemnify or reimburse another for loss that occurs under the terms of the contract.

Interest- The charge for borrowing money or the return for lending it.

Interest bearing account- https://www. bankinter.com/banca/en/financial-dictionary/ interest-bearing-account#:

An interest-bearing account is a type of bank account that pays the customer an interest rate in exchange for them depositing their money at the bank. The return and interest rate offered will vary by bank and depend on the account terms and conditions. They can also change over time.

1. Landlord- a person or organization that owns and leases apartments to others. A person who owns and leases land, buildings, etc.

Loan- something lent or furnished on condition of being returned, especially a sum of money lent at interest: *a $1000 loan at 10 percent interest.* To lend (money) at interest.

Matching funds- https://en.wikipedia.org/ wiki/Matching_funds

Matching funds are funds that are set to be paid in proportion to funds available from other sources. Matching fund payments usually arise in situations of charity or public good.

Mortgage- the total loan obtained or the periodic installment to be paid under such a transaction: *They took out a $500,000 mortgage.* The obligation to repay such a loan; the debt incurred.

Possess- to have as belonging to one; have as property; own: to possess a house and a car.

Real estate agent- https://www.investopedia.com/terms/r/realestateagent.asp

A real estate agent is a licensed professional who arranges real estate transactions, putting buyers and sellers together and acting as their representative in negotiations. Real estate agents usually are compensated completely by a commission. In almost every state a real estate agent must work for or be affiliated with a real estate broker (an individual or a brokerage firm), who is more experienced and licensed to a higher degree.

Wealth- *as relating to Economics.*

1. all things that have a monetary or exchange value.
2. anything that has utility and is capable of being appropriated or exchanged.

Lightning Source UK Ltd.
Milton Keynes UK
UKHW021119281222
414477UK00001B/15

That's My House

Due to the changing nature of the Internet, if there are any web addresses, links, or URLs included in this manuscript, these may have been altered and may no longer be accessible. The views and opinions shared in this book belong solely to the author and do not necessarily reflect those of the publisher. The publisher therefore disclaims responsibility for the views or opinions expressed within the work.